8/6/93

Dear Pia,
Hope you'll love
this book, enjoy
reading it! Happy-Bday!
love,
Tita Annie
Tito Jojo
Arlene + Tony

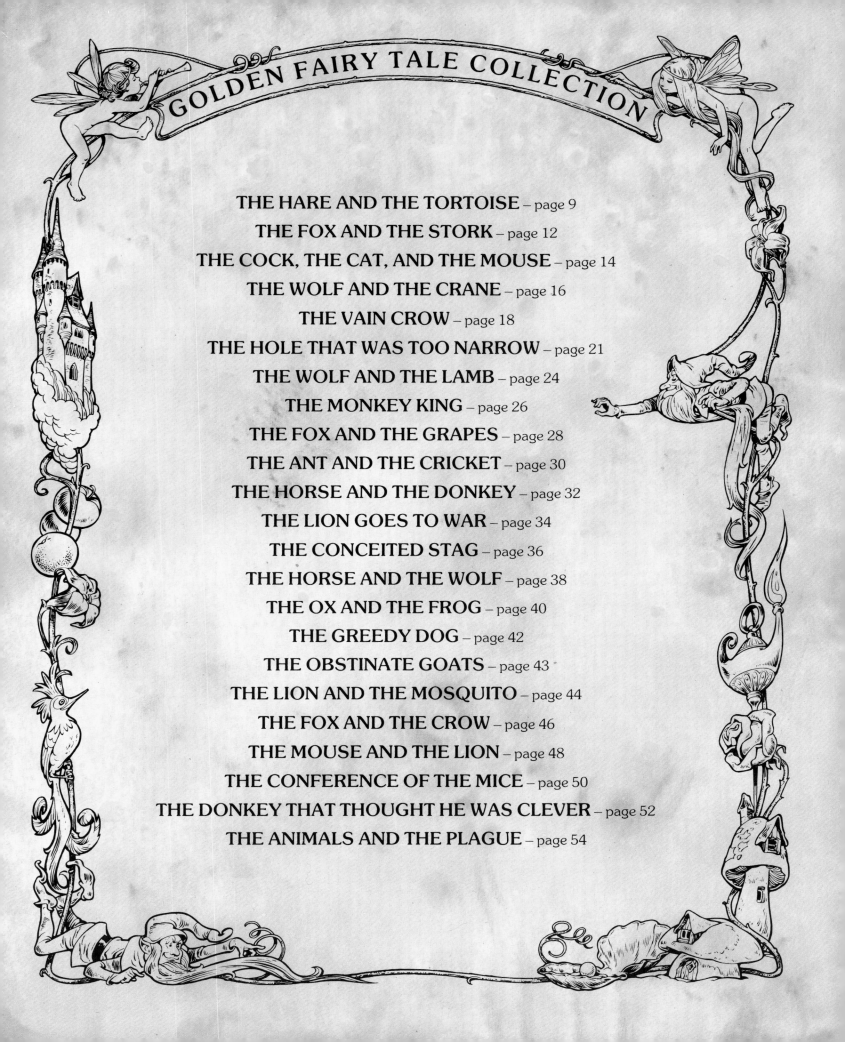

GOLDEN FAIRY TALE COLLECTION

ILLUSTRATED BY TONY WOLF
TEXT BY PETER HOLEINONE

First published in the United States 1990
by Gallery Books, an imprint of W. H. Smith Publishers, Inc.,
112 Madison Avenue, New York, New York 10016.

Gallery Books are available for bulk purchase for sales
promotions and premium use. For details write or telephone
the Manager of Special Sales, W. H. Smith Publishers, Inc.,
112 Madison Avenue, New York, New York 10016. (212) 532-6600

 PRINTED BY
ARTI GRAFICHE MOTTA
MILANO - ITALY

The story of
THE HARE AND THE TORTOISE
and other tales

GALLERY BOOKS
An Imprint of W. H. Smith Publishers Inc.
112 Madison Avenue
New York, New York 10016

Once upon a time . . .

. . . a conceited hare challenged a long-suffering tortoise to an absurd race. And, incredible though it may seem to you, this is the story . . .

THE HARE AND THE TORTOISE

Once upon a time . . . . there was a hare who, boasting how he could run faster than anyone else, was forever teasing a tortoise for its slowness. Then one day, the irate tortoise answered back: "Who do you think you are? There's no denying you're swift, but even you can be beaten!" The hare squealed with laughter.

"Beaten in a race? By whom? Not you, surely! I bet there's nobody in the world that can win against me, I'm so speedy. Now, why don't you try?"

Annoyed by such bragging, the tortoise accepted the challenge. A course was planned, and next day at dawn they stood at the starting line. The hare yawned sleepily as the meek tortoise trudged slowly off. When the hare saw how painfully slow his rival was, he decided, half asleep on his feet, to have a quick nap. "Take your time!" he said. "I'll have forty winks and catch up with you in a minute."

The hare woke with a start from a fitful sleep and gazed round, looking for the tortoise. But the creature was only a short distance away, having barely covered a third of the course. Breathing a sigh of relief, the hare decided he might as well have breakfast too, and off he went to munch some cabbages he had noticed in a nearby field. But the heavy meal and the hot sun made his eyelids droop. With a careless glance at the tortoise, now halfway along the course, he decided to have another snooze before flashing past the winning post. And smiling at the thought of the look on the tortoise's face when it saw the hare speed by, he fell fast asleep and was soon snoring happily. The sun started to sink below the horizon, and the tortoise, who had been plodding towards the winning post since morning, was scarcely a yard from the finish. At that very point, the hare woke with a jolt. He could see the tortoise a speck in the distance and away he dashed. He leapt and bounded at a great rate, his tongue lolling, and gasping for breath. Just a little more and he'd be first at the finish. But the hare's last leap was just too late, for the tortoise had beaten him to the winning post. Poor hare! Tired and in disgrace, he slumped down beside the tortoise who was silently smiling at him.

"Slowly does it every time!" he said.

THE FOX
AND THE STORK

Once upon a time . . . a fox made friends with a stork and decided to invite her to lunch. While he was wondering what to serve for the meal, he thought he'd play a trick on the bird. So he prepared a tasty soup and poured it into two flat plates.

"Help yourself, Mrs Stork! I'm sure you'll enjoy this! It's frog soup and chopped parsley. Taste it, you'll find it's delicious!"

"Thank you very much!" said the stork, sniffing the soup. But she quickly saw the trick the fox had played on her. For no matter how she tried, she could not drink the soup from the flat plate. The sniggering fox urged her on: "Eat up! Do you like it?" But all the stork could do was bluff. With a casual air she said: "I'm afraid I've such a headache that I've lost my appetite!" And the fox fussily replied: "What a shame! And it's such good soup too! Too bad! Maybe next time . . ." To which the stork quickly replied: "Yes, of course! Next time, you must have lunch with me!"

The very next day, the fox found a polite note pinned to his door: it was the stork's invitation to lunch. "Now, isn't that nice of her!" said the fox to himself. "And she hasn't taken my little trick to heart either! A real lady!"

The stork's house was much plainer than the fox's, and she apologised to the fox. "My home is much humbler than yours," she said, "but I've cooked a really special meal. Freshwater shrimps with white wine and juniper berries!" The fox licked his lips at the idea of these goodies and sniffed deeply when the stork handed him his jar. But, try as he might, he was unable to eat a bite, for he could not reach down with his nose into the long neck of the jar. In the meantime, with her long beak, the stork gobbled her lunch. "Try it! Try it!" she said. "Do you like it?" But the unlucky fox, confused and outsmarted, could not think of an excuse for not eating.

And as he tossed and turned hungrily in bed that night, thinking of his lost lunch, he said to himself with a sigh: "I might have known!"

THE COCK, THE CAT, AND THE MOUSE

Once upon a time . . . a little mouse decided to go and see the world. Packing some food for the journey, he carefully locked his door and set off for the unknown. And what a wonderful world he saw! Tall trees, rolling countryside, flowers and butterflies he had never set eyes on before. On he hiked till, tired out, he came to a peasant's cottage. After eating some of his packed lunch, he thought he would inspect what, to him, was a peculiar sort of building. He entered the farmyard and his eyes grew round as saucers: there in front of him were two strange animals he had never seen before. One was large and handsome, with four legs, covered all over with soft fur, and sporting splendid white whiskers that gave it a solemn respectable air. It was dozing against the wall. The other, a two-legged creature, had red, yellow and green feathers and a fierce, bad-tempered look. A pair of cruel eyes

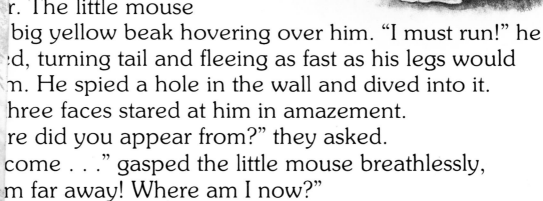

...crested head
...the little mouse.
...do you do, sir!
...you do . . ."
...e mouse's
...as he felt foolish
...owing the
...s name. But the
...d creature simply
...ut its chest,
...d a loud "Cock-
...e-doo!" and
...towards the
...now paralysed
...r. The little mouse
...big yellow beak hovering over him. "I must run!" he
...d, turning tail and fleeing as fast as his legs would
...m. He spied a hole in the wall and dived into it.
...hree faces stared at him in amazement.
...re did you appear from?" they asked.
...come . . ." gasped the little mouse breathlessly,
...m far away! Where am I now?"
"This is our home. We're field mice. What happened?" And
the little mouse told them about the animals he had met in
the farmyard: one handsome and harmless, the other brightly
coloured and ferocious.   The three field mice laughed.
"Calm down," they said. "Have a cup of coffee. Don't you
realise the danger you were in? The creature that frightened
you is only a cock, but the nice harmless one is our deadliest
enemy, the cat! If he'd seen you, you wouldn't be here to tell
the tale. As you see, you can't always judge by appearances!"

THE WOLF AND THE CRANE

Once upon a time . . . a wolf well known for his ferocity received his punishment for being greedy. As he was devouring a lamb, a tiny sharp bone stuck in his throat. And from that day on, he could swallow nothing except sips of water, which neither soothed the pain nor appeased his hunger. Though he tried every remedy he knew, he was unable to dislodge the bone. In despair, he started to ask everyone he knew for help. But, scared of his awful reputation, folk made excuses to avoid the wolf and would have nothing to do with him. One day, from behind his barred door, the fox said: "I'm not well, so I can't open the door, but I think you ought to have a word with the crane down at the end of the big pond. Folk say she's the best doctor around here."

Without much hope and feeling sorry for himself, the wolf went to see the crane. And when he got to her house, he tried his best to be pleasant.

"Mrs Crane, I'm told you're enormously clever. If you can help me, I'll give you a rich reward!"

At first, the crane, well aware of the wolf's reputation, was alarmed, though also proud at the idea of treating such a famous patient. And, attracted too by the promise of a reward, she said she'd see what she could do.

The wolf opened wide his huge mouth. The crane shuddered at the thought of peering inside the red jaws with their sharp fangs, but plucking up her courage, she said: "Now, please keep your mouth wide open, or I won't be able to remove the bone!" And she poked her long beak down the wolf's throat and pulled out the little bone.

"There! You can close your mouth again. You'll be able to swallow whatever you like now!" The wolf could hardly believe it. His throat was clear at last! Highly delighted, the crane said: "See how clever I am? You didn't feel a thing! I whipped out that nasty bone with my long beak! And as for my

reward . . ." The wolf interrupted with a scowl.

"Reward? What reward? You ought to be grateful that I didn't bite your head off while it was down my throat! You should give *me* a reward for sparing your life!"

Seeing the wolf's bloodshot eyes, the crane realised she was now in danger. What more could she expect from such a wicked wolf? And she vowed that, from then on, she'd only treat patients too harmless ever to threaten her.

THE VAIN CROW

Once upon a time . . . a restless crow decided to go farther away than usual from home and friends. Suddenly, in a farmyard, he met a pair of peacocks. What wonderful birds they were! The crow had never seen such beautiful feathers, and he timidly asked the regal-looking birds what they were.

"We're peacocks," one of them replied, spreading its tail. And as the peacock strutted about, showing the crow his magnificent feathers, he screamed, as peacocks do. Bursting with admiration, the crow said goodbye and flapped away, but as he flew home, he could not forget the two peacocks. "What fine feathers! They must be so happy, being so beautiful." And he gazed down sadly at his own ugly plumes. From that day on, he could not help thinking about the splendour of the peacocks and his own plain feathers. He even stopped looking at himself in the pond water, for every time he did so, it made him even more depressed. He got into the habit of spying on the peacocks, and the more he watched them strut royally around, the more envious he was of their beauty.

One day, he noticed that one of the peacocks had dropped a feather. When the sun went down, the crow picked it up and hid it away. For days on end, he watched the peacocks and found another feather. When he had four, he could wait no longer: he stuck the peacock feathers onto his own tail, using pine resin, and started to parade up and down for his friends to admire.

"Just look at my gorgeous tail!" he said proudly.

"I'm not ugly like you! Out of my way, you moth eaten crows!" The crows' amazement soon changed to indignation, then they started to laugh and jeer at their vain companion. "You're nothing but a crow yourself, even with those flashy feathers!" they jeered.

"And you're silly as well as ugly," replied the conceited crow haughtily, and off he went to live with the peacocks. When the peacocks set eyes on the stranger, they thought the crow was just another peacock who, for some reason, had lost most of his feathers, and they felt sorry for him. But the crow, vainer than ever, wanted to attract greater admiration and a foolish idea came into his head. He tried to scream the way the peacocks do when they fan their tails. But the harsh "Craw! Craw! Craw!" quickly betrayed the crow. The furious peacocks pecked the stolen feathers off and chased the crow away. Poor crow! For when, sad and downcast, he went back to his friends, he was given exactly the same rough treatment. Nobody would speak to him and all the crows turned their backs on him for trying to be what he was not.

THE HOLE THAT WAS TOO NARROW

Once upon a time . . . a stoat
was so greedy that he would
eat anything that came his
way. But he was punished
for his greed. He found some
old stale eggs in a barn and,
as usual, gobbled the lot.
However, he soon started to
feel agonising pains in his
tummy, his eyes grew dim
and he broke out in a cold
sweat. For days, he lay between life and death, then the fever
dropped. The first time he dared climb a tree to rob a nest,
thin and weak, with his trousers dangling over an empty
stomach, he became dizzy and fell. That is how he twisted his
ankle. Sick with hunger, he limped about in search of food,
but that made him feel even hungrier than before. Then good
luck came his way. Although wary of venturing too close to
human habitations, he was so hungry he went up to a tavern
on the outskirts of the village. The air was full of lovely smells
and the poor stoat felt his mouth watering as he pictured all
the nice things inside. An inviting smell coming from a crack
in the wall seemed to be stronger than the others. Thrusting
his nose into the crack, he was greeted by a waft of delicious
scents. The stoat frantically clawed at the crack with his paws
and teeth, trying to widen it. Slowly the plaster between the
blocks of rubble began to crumble, till all he had to do was
move a stone. Shoving with all his might, the stoat made a
hole. And then a *really* wonderful sight met his gaze. He was
inside the pantry, where hams, salamis, cheeses, honey, jam
and nuts were stored. Overwhelmed by it all, the stoat could

not make up his mind what to taste first. He jumped from one thing to another, munching all the time, till his tummy was full. Satisfied at last, he fell asleep. Then he woke again, had another feast and went back to sleep. With all this food, his strength returned, and next day, the stoat was strong enough to climb up to the topmost shelves and select the tastiest delicacies. By this time, he was just having a nibble here and a nibble there. But he never stopped eating: he went on and on and on. By now, he was very full indeed, as he chattered to himself: ''Salami for starters . . . no, the ham's better! Some soft cheese and a spot of mature cheese as well . . . I think I'll have a pickled sausage too . . .''

In only a few days, the stoat had become very fat and his trouser button had popped off over a bulging tummy. But of course, the stoat's fantastic luck could not last for ever.

One afternoon, the stoat froze in mid-munch at the creak of a door. Heavy footsteps thumped down the stairs, and the stoat looked helplessly round. Fear of discovery sent him hunting for a way to escape. He ran towards the hole in the wall through which he had come. But though his head and shoulders entered the hole, his tummy, which had grown much larger since the day he had come in, simply would not pass. The stoat was in a dangerous position: he was stuck! Two thick hands grabbed him by the tail.

''You horrid little robber! So you thought you'd get away, did you? I'll soon deal with you!''

Strange though it may sound, the only thought in the greedy stoat's head was a longing to be starving of hunger again . . .

THE WOLF AND THE LAMB

Once upon a time . . . in the forest lived a wolf, known to be savage and ruthless. One day, feeling thirsty, the wolf went down to a stream, and as he drank the sparkling water, he saw a lamb drinking, further downstream. The minute he set eyes on the hapless lamb, he decided to make a meal of it. "A nice plump lamb! Fine and tender! Yummy! That will be delicious! I haven't had such luck in ages! Now, I must find an excuse for picking a quarrel, so that nobody can accuse me of gobbling it unjustly!"

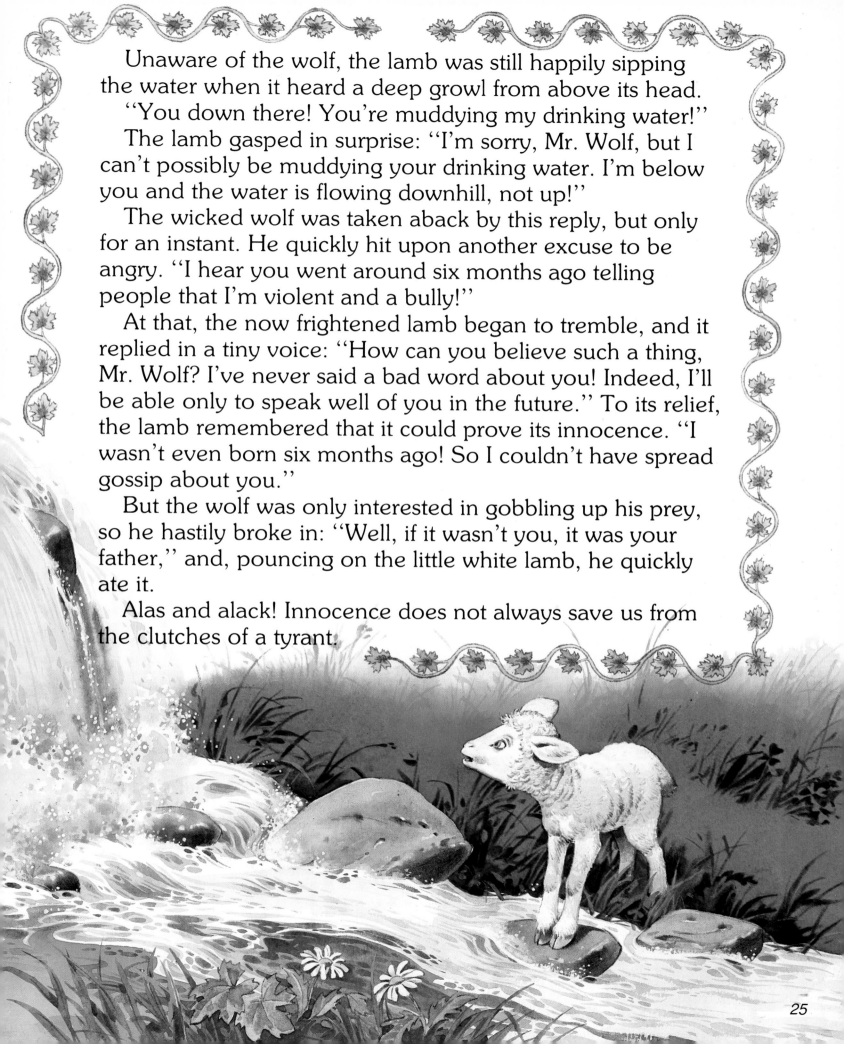

Unaware of the wolf, the lamb was still happily sipping the water when it heard a deep growl from above its head.

"You down there! You're muddying my drinking water!"

The lamb gasped in surprise: "I'm sorry, Mr. Wolf, but I can't possibly be muddying your drinking water. I'm below you and the water is flowing downhill, not up!"

The wicked wolf was taken aback by this reply, but only for an instant. He quickly hit upon another excuse to be angry. "I hear you went around six months ago telling people that I'm violent and a bully!"

At that, the now frightened lamb began to tremble, and it replied in a tiny voice: "How can you believe such a thing, Mr. Wolf? I've never said a bad word about you! Indeed, I'll be able only to speak well of you in the future." To its relief, the lamb remembered that it could prove its innocence. "I wasn't even born six months ago! So I couldn't have spread gossip about you."

But the wolf was only interested in gobbling up his prey, so he hastily broke in: "Well, if it wasn't you, it was your father," and, pouncing on the little white lamb, he quickly ate it.

Alas and alack! Innocence does not always save us from the clutches of a tyrant.

THE MONKEY KING

Once upon a time . . . a long time
ago, there was a thick jungle
where many kinds of animals lived
in harmony together. Their ruler
was a wise old lion. But one sad
day, the king died and the animals
had to decide who was to be their new ruler. The dead king
had a gold crown, encrusted with precious gems, and it was
decided that all the candidates for the throne were to come
forward and each would try on the crown, and the ruler
would be the animal whose head it fitted. Now, though many
tried on the crown, it fitted no-one. Some heads were too big,
others too small, a few had horns and some had big ears. The
fact was that the old king's crown did not fit any of the
animals. Then a cheeky monkey snatched up the crown and
started to amuse the crowd with clever tricks. First, he slipped
the crown round his waist and whirled it round and round his
middle without letting it fall to the ground. Then he
tossed it higher and higher into the air and caught it as
it came down. He then stood on his head and twirled
the crown on the tips of his toes, before jumping to
his feet again and catching it in his hands. All the
animals laughed delightedly at the nimble monkey's
skill and clapped in excitement. Pleased at the great
applause, the monkey went on with his show, till
the enthusiastic crowd decided to award him the
crown and proclaim him king.

The only animal to disagree was the fox.
"A silly creature like that can't be our king!"
he said. "I'm going to do all I can to make
him lose the throne."

One day, having just managed to avoid a trap that men had set at the edge of the jungle, the fox took it unseen to the tree where the monkey lived. Covering the trap with dead leaves, the fox picked a large bunch of bananas and called up to the monkey: "Sire! Sire! Can you help me? I have some ripe bananas I'd like to present you with, but I can't climb trees as easily as you do! Would you please come down and accept my gift?" The unsuspecting monkey shinned down the tree, and just as he reached for the bananas, the trap suddenly clamped shut over his legs. The fox began to laugh: "What a foolish king we have! Fancy falling into a trap for a handful of bananas!" And calling all the other animals, he went on: "Just look at our sovereign! Isn't he stupid? He can't even avoid being caught in a trap. If he isn't able to watch out for himself, how can we expect him to look after us?" All the animals let themselves be persuaded by the fox's words, and in a twinkling the monkey king was deprived of the crown. And from that day on, this particular jungle was the only one whose animals made do without a king.

THE FOX AND THE GRAPES

Once upon a time . . . in a wood there lived a very crafty quick-witted fox. The rabbits, rats, the birds and all the other creatures fled at the sight of him, for they all knew how cruel and famished he was. And since his prey kept fearfully out of sight, the fox had no choice but to haunt the neighbourhood buildings in the hope of finding something to eat. The first time, he was in luck. Near a lonely peasant's cottage, only a low fence stood between him and the hen run, and there he left death and destruction behind him.

"What careless men, leaving such tender fat hens unguarded," he said to himself as he trotted away, still munching.

A few days later, hungry once more, he decided to visit the same hen run again. He crept up to the fence. A thread of smoke curled from the cottage chimney, but all was quiet. With a great bound, he leapt into the hen run. The cackling hens scattered, and the fox was already clutching one in his jaws when a stone hit him on the side.

"Wicked brute!" yelled a man waving a stick. "Now I've got you!"

To make matters worse, up raced a large dog, snarling viciously. The fox dropped the hen and tried to jump out of the

hen run. At the first try, he fell back, perhaps weak with fright. He could almost feel the dog's fangs sink into his ear, but with a desperate jump, he got over the fence. The yells and stones streamed after the bruised fox as he ran into the wood. In a nearby glade, he glanced round to make sure that he was not being followed. "Bad luck!" he said to himself. "All those hens . . ." His mouth was watering and he could feel gnawing hunger pains. Right above his head stretched a vine, laden with bunches of big ripe grapes. "Well, if there's nothing else . . ." muttered the fox, jumping up towards the grapes. But the bunches were hanging just beyond his reach. The fox then took a running jump at them, but without success. And though he tried over and over again, the grapes remained beyond his grasp.

"Craw! Craw! Craw!" laughed a crow overhead, mocking the disappointed fox.

"Sour grapes!" exclaimed the fox loudly. 'I'll come back when they're ripe." And thrusting out his chest to give himself airs, though still smarting from the blows he had received, he set off towards the woods with an empty stomach.

29

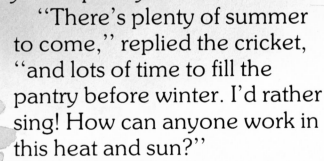

THE ANT AND THE CRICKET

Once upon a time . . . one hot summer, a cricket sang cheerfully on the branch of a tree, while down below, a long line of ants struggled gamely under the weight of their load of grains; and between one song and the next, the cricket spoke to the ants. "Why are you working so hard? Come into the shade, away from the sun, and sing a song with me." But the tireless ants went on with their work . . . "We can't do that," they said. "We must store away food for the winter. When the weather's cold and the ground white with snow, there's nothing to eat, and we'll survive the winter only if the pantry is full."

"There's plenty of summer to come," replied the cricket, "and lots of time to fill the pantry before winter. I'd rather sing! How can anyone work in this heat and sun?"

And so, all summer, the cricket sang while the ants laboured. But the days turned into weeks and the weeks into months. Autumn came, the leaves began to fall and the cricket left the bare tree. The grass too was turning thin and yellow. One morning, the cricket woke shivering with cold. An early frost tinged the fields with white and turned the last of the green leaves brown: winter had come at last. The cricket wandered, feeding on the few dry stalks left on the hard frozen ground. Then the snow fell and she could find nothing at all to eat. Trembling and famished, she thought sadly of the warmth and her summer songs. One evening, she saw a speck of light in the distance, and trampling through the thick snow, made her way towards it.

"Open the door! Please open the door! I'm starving! Give me some food!" An ant leant out of the window.

"Who's there? Who is it?"

"It's me – the cricket. I'm cold and hungry, with no roof over my head."

"The cricket? Ah, yes! I remember you. And what were you doing all summer while we were getting ready for winter?"

"Me? I was singing and filling the whole earth and sky with my song!"

"Singing, eh?" said the ant. "Well, try dancing now!"

THE HORSE AND THE DONKEY

Once upon a time . . . an old carter kept a horse and a donkey in the same stable. He was equally fond of both his animals, but as he used the horse to pull his trap, he gave it better food and more attention than he did the donkey. However, the donkey, knowing he was not so precious as his stablemate, ate straw instead of corn and hay, without complaining. Even when both animals carried sacks to market, the donkey's was the heavier load, for the carter did not want to overwork his noble horse, though he had no such feelings about the donkey. As time went by, the horse grew more handsome and robust, while the donkey became thin and weak. One day, on their way to market, the donkey was carrying his usual heavy load, while the horse had only two lightweight sacks tied to the saddle.

"I can't go much further!" moaned the donkey. "I'm much weaker today! I can hardly stand and unless I can get rid of some of this weight, I won't be able to go on. Couldn't you take some of my load?"

When the horse heard this, he looked the donkey up and down in disdain, for he considered himself much superior, and said: "Our master gave you the heavy load, because he knows that donkeys are beasts of burden. Their loads ought to be heavier than those of noble horses!"

So the wretched donkey stumbled on. But after a short distance, he stopped again, bleary-eyed, his tongue hanging out.

"Please, please listen! If you don't help me, I'll never reach market alive." But without even a glance, the horse haughtily replied: "Rubbish! Come on, you'll manage this time too!"

But this time, after a few tottering steps, the donkey dropped dead to the ground. The donkey's master, who had lingered to pick mushrooms, ran up when he saw the animal fall.

"Poor thing!" he said. "He served me well for so many years. His load must have been too heavy."

Then he turned to the horse: "Come here! You'll have to carry your companion's load too now!" And he hoisted the donkey's sacks onto the horse's back.

"I'd have done better to help the donkey when he was alive," said the horse to himself. "A little more weight wouldn't have done me any harm. Now, I'm frightened of collapsing myself under a double load!" But feeling sorry too late did nothing to lighten his load.

THE LION GOES TO WAR

Once upon a time . . . a lion decided to go to war. He summoned his ministers, and called together his army with this proclamation: "King Lion commands that all animals in the forest must come before him tomorrow to go to war. Nobody must fail to appear."

The lion's subjects all presented themselves punctually and the lion issued the orders: "Elephant, you're the largest, you'll transport the guns and all the supplies. You, fox, have a reputation for cunning, so you'll help me draw up the plans of battle to beat off enemy attacks. You, monkey, nimble and good at climbing trees, will act as lookout and spy the enemy's movements from above. Bear, you're strong and agile, so you'll scale the fortress walls and terrorize the enemy."

Amongst those present were also the rabbit and the donkey. When the king's ministers saw them, they shook their heads, then one said: "Sire, I don't think the donkey will make a good soldier. They say he's easily frightened."

The lion looked at the donkey, then turning to his ministers, He remarked:

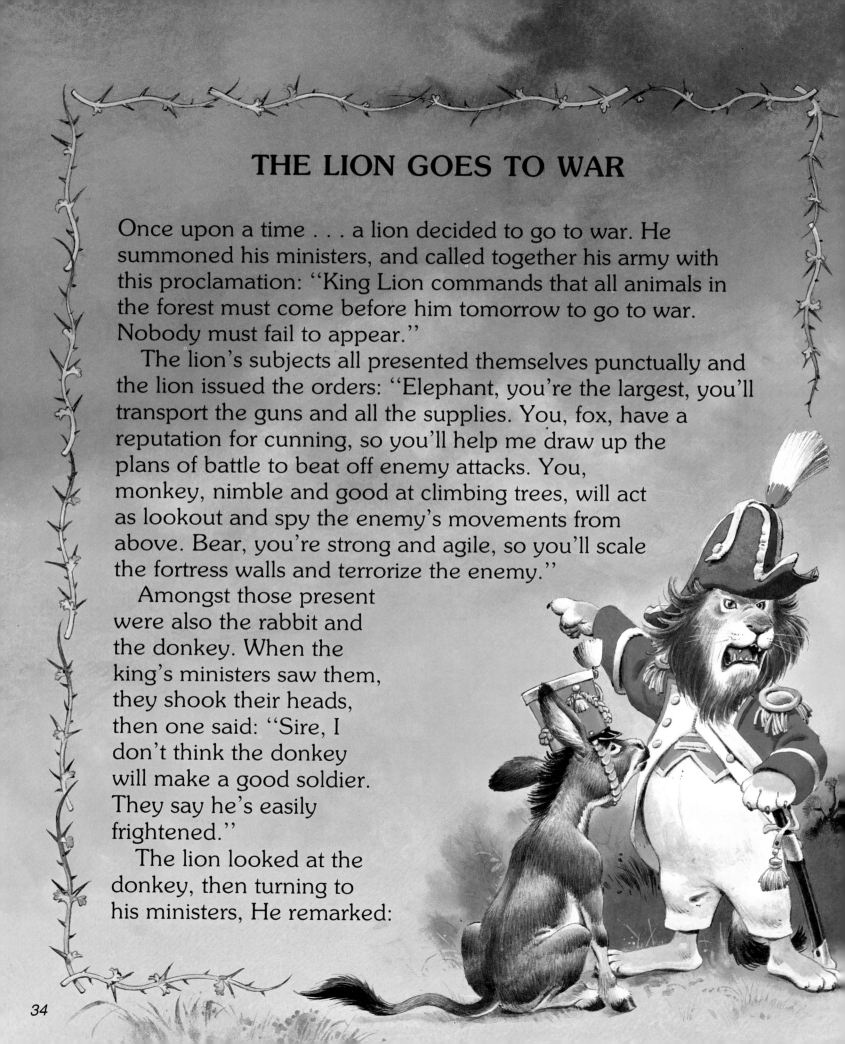

"He brays louder than I can roar. He'll stay at my side and be the trumpet that will rally the troops."

The ministers then pointed to the rabbit: "He's even more nervous than the donkey. We should send him home!"

Again the lion stood thoughtfully for a moment, then going over to the rabbit, he said: "You always flee from your enemies, so you've learned that you have to be faster than the others if you're to survive. So you'll act as messenger, and within seconds, all the soldiers will receive my orders." Then, turning to the crowd, he said: "Everyone can make himself useful in a war; everyone can help the common cause as best he is able!"

THE CONCEITED STAG

Once upon a time . . . there was a stag with splendidly long antlers, who was very conceited. Every time he drank at a pool, he would stand and admire his reflection in the water. "I am handsome," he would tell himself. "There's no finer set of antlers in the forest!" And off he would prance. Like all stags, he had long slender legs, but folk said he'd rather break a leg than lose a single branch of his splendid antlers. Poor foolish stag! How vain he was.

One day, as he grazed peacefully on the tender shoots on some low branches, he heard a distant shot.

He heard with fear the baying of the hounds. Terrified, he knew what terrible enemies the hounds were and that, if they caught his scent, it would not be easy to outrun them.

He had to flee, at once, and as quickly as possible. Faster and faster, he sped along the woodland track, his heart in his mouth. He could hear the baying of the pack at his heels. Without ever looking back, he ran in a straight line, trying to shake off his pursuers. Then the wood thinned out into a clearing. "With luck, I'll be safe now," he said to himself, running swiftly over the smooth ground. And indeed, the yelping of the hounds seemed to die away in the distance.

Only a little further now, and the stag would reach safety. Suddenly, as he swept under a tree, his antlers caught in the low-hanging branches. He shook his head desperately, trying to break free, but although he struggled, his antlers were held fast. The hounds were coming closer and closer. Just before the stag met his doom, he had time to think: "What a mistake I made in regarding my antlers as the best and most precious part of my body. I should have had more respect for my legs. They tried to carry me to safety, while my antlers will be the death of me!"

THE HORSE AND THE WOLF

Once upon a time . . . a horse was grazing peacefully in a rolling green meadow. A famished wolf passing by saw the horse and his mouth began to water.

"That's a fine horse! And will taste good too! He'd make a juicy steak! Pity he's so big, I don't think I'd manage to bring him down, though you never know . . ."

The wolf approached the horse, which continued to eat the grass. ". . . maybe, if I take him by surprise."

Now quite close, the wolf spoke to the horse, trying to sound as pleasant as he could.

"Good day, Mr. Horse, I see you're enjoying a meal. Is the grass good? I must say you're looking rather pale. Aren't you well?"

His mouth full of grass, the horse replied: "Pale? Oh, no, that's my natural colour. I was born white and grey."

The wolf pretended not to understand what the horse had said. "Yes, indeed, very pale. It's just as well your master has given you a holiday in the field, instead of working."

"A holiday in the field? But I'm the picture of health! . . ."

The wolf was now circling round the horse, trying to find the best point of attack.

"I'm a doctor," he went on. "I can treat you. If you tell me where the pain is, I'm sure I can cure it. Take my advice. Let me examine you!"

The horse, who was not usually wary of others, became suspicious of the wolf's persistent remarks, and thought he had better be on his guard. The wolf was now very close and carefully biding his time, when the horse said, in alarm: "Yes! Now that I think of it, I have a sore hind foot. It's been swollen for ages . . ."

Without a moment's thought, the wolf trotted up to the hoof which the horse had obligingly raised into the air. And when he was certain that the wolf had come within range, the horse gave a mighty kick, catching the wolf on the jawbone and sending him flying.

"Would you like to examine me again?" The wolf heard the words as he struggled to his feet with spinning head.

"No thanks! That's enough for one day!" he mumbled, limping away, with no further thought for horse steaks.

THE OX
AND THE FROG

Once upon a time . . . a conceited frog never missed an opportunity to show his friends how different he was, and how much better than everyone else. When folk were jumping, he always tried to do the highest jump, when it was a question of diving, he was first into the water. In other words, he had to be tops all the time. One day, a big ox came to drink at the pond. Frightened, all the frogs hopped away to hide in the reeds, but when they saw that the ox was harmless, they came out again to watch the huge beast. "Isn't he whopping!" they exclaimed to each other. One frog then said: "It would take hundreds of frogs like us to make one of him!"

Now, the conceited frog, far more scared than the others, had dived into the water at the sight of the ox. But a little later he returned and, after listening to his friends' remarks, he said: "He's certainly bigger than we are. But he's not *enormous*!"

But nobody was paying any attention to the conceited frog, so he raised his voice . . . and puffing out his chest, announced: "I could easily become as big as that ox! Look!"

The frogs began to smirk. "You're very little, far too little!" But the frog just blew himself out even more. "Now look," he whispered, as he tried not to lose air. His friends giggled. "What about now?" he managed to gasp, as he blew some more. "The ox is much bigger," came the reply. The conceited frog made a last great effort: taking an extra deep breath, he blew himself up until . . . BANG! His skin burst! The astonished frogs saw their friend disappear from sight, for nothing was left of the conceited frog but scraps of green skin. The ox, who had raised his head when he heard the bang, went back to his drinking, and the frogs hopped away, remarking: "It doesn't do to become too swollen-headed . . ."

THE GREEDY DOG

Once upon a time . . . a dog managed to steal a large steak from a butcher's shop, and ran into the woods to eat it in peace. On reaching the banks of a stream, he happened to see his face reflected in the water. Never for a moment thinking that he was looking at himself in the water, what he thought he saw was another dog, holding a large steak in its mouth.

Being a greedy dog, he jumped into the stream to snatch the other dog's meat. Of course, the reflection vanished and he could see no sign of dog or steak.

Only then did he realise that, when he barked to frighten the other, he had dropped his stolen meat. Unluckily for him, the current was swift and the steak had been carried away. And though the dog hunted all over, he couldn't find a trace of it. Which meant, that instead of having two steaks, he was left with nothing.

THE OBSTINATE GOATS

Once upon a time . . . two mountain goats happened to be going down the opposite slopes of a valley, through which flowed a rushing river.

Now, some of the mountain dwellers had bridged the river by placing a large tree trunk that had been struck by lightning, to join the steep rocky banks.

The two goats met head on half way across the tree trunk for each wanted to cross to the other side. But the trunk was not nearly wide enough for them to pass each other, and neither goat was inclined to give way. Obstinately, they began to bicker, but neither would budge an inch. Words soon led to action and they started to fight, till finally both tumbled off the tree trunk into the river below. Wouldn't it have been much simpler if only one of the goats had been courteous enough to allow the other to pass?

THE LION AND THE MOSQUITO

Once upon a time . . . a tiny mosquito started to buzz round a lion he met. "Go away!" grumbled the sleepy lion, smacking his own cheek in an attempt to drive the insect away.

"Why should I?" demanded the mosquito. "You're king of the jungle, not of the air! I'll fly wherever I want and land wherever I please." And so saying, he tickled the lion's ear. In the hope of crushing the insect, the lion boxed his own ears, but the mosquito slipped away from the now dazed lion.

"I don't feel it any more. Either it's squashed or it's gone away." But at that very moment, the irritating buzz began again, and the mosquito flew into the lion's nose. Wild with rage, the lion leapt to his hind legs and started to rain punches on his own nose. But the insect, safe inside, refused to budge. With a swollen nose and watery eyes, the lion gave a terrific sneeze, blasting the mosquito out. Angry at being dislodged so abruptly, the mosquito returned to the attack: BUZZ . . . BUZZZ! . . . it whizzed round the lion's head. Large and tough as the lion was, he could not rid himself of his tiny tormenter. This made him angrier still, and he roared fiercely. At the sound of his terrible voice, all the forest creatures fled in fear, but paying no heed to the exhausted lion, the mosquito said triumphantly: "There you are, king of the jungle! Foiled by a tiny mosquito like me!" And highly delighted with his victory, off he buzzed. But he did not notice a spider's web hanging close by, and soon he was turning and twisting, trying to escape from the trap set by a large spider. "Bah!" said the spider in disgust, as he ate it. "Another tiny mosquito. Not much to get excited about, but better than nothing. I was hoping for something more substantial . . ."

And that's what became of the mosquito that foiled the lion!

THE FOX AND THE CROW

Once upon a time . . . a big crow stole a lump of cheese and went to perch on a branch of a tree to eat it in peace. A passing fox sniffed the air and stopped below the tree, his mouth watering.

"Cheese?" he said. "Mmm. I'd love . . . if only I could . . ." he said to himself, greedily, wondering how to get hold of the morsel.

After a moment or two, he spoke to the crow: "You *are* a fine crow! I've never seen anyone so big and strong. What lovely thick shiny feathers you have! And such slender legs, the sign of a noble bird. And a regal beak. That's it: the beak of a king! You ought to be crowned King of the Birds!"

When the crow heard such glowing praise of his beauty, he stretched to his full length and triumphantly flapped his wings.

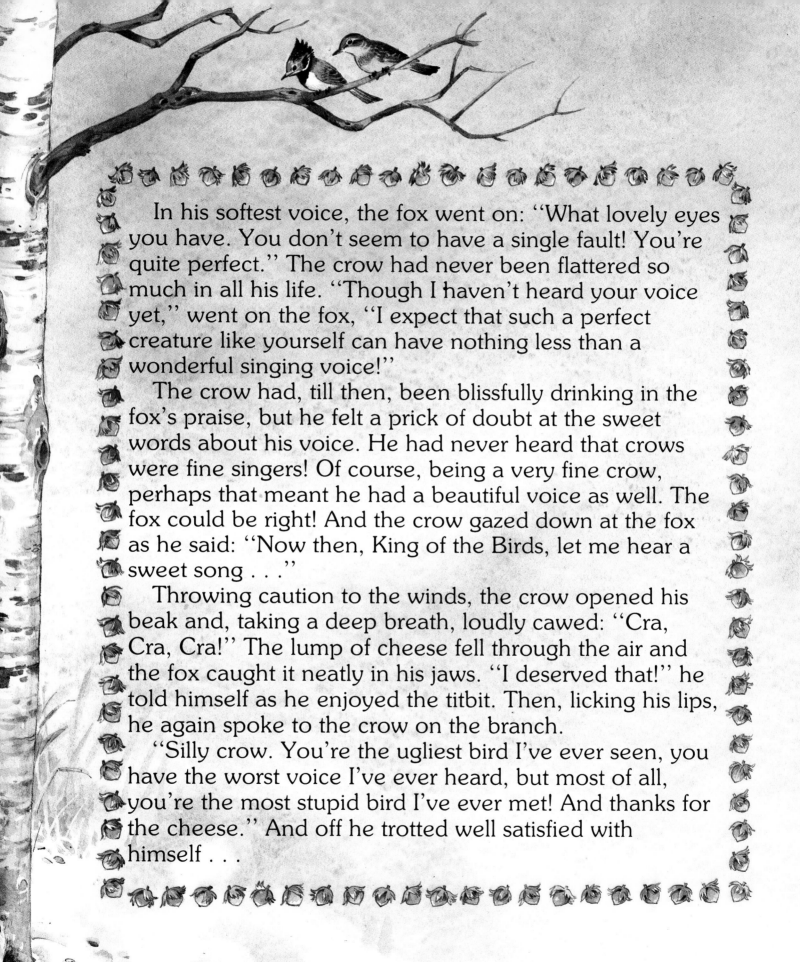

In his softest voice, the fox went on: "What lovely eyes you have. You don't seem to have a single fault! You're quite perfect." The crow had never been flattered so much in all his life. "Though I haven't heard your voice yet," went on the fox, "I expect that such a perfect creature like yourself can have nothing less than a wonderful singing voice!"

The crow had, till then, been blissfully drinking in the fox's praise, but he felt a prick of doubt at the sweet words about his voice. He had never heard that crows were fine singers! Of course, being a very fine crow, perhaps that meant he had a beautiful voice as well. The fox could be right! And the crow gazed down at the fox as he said: "Now then, King of the Birds, let me hear a sweet song . . ."

Throwing caution to the winds, the crow opened his beak and, taking a deep breath, loudly cawed: "Cra, Cra, Cra!" The lump of cheese fell through the air and the fox caught it neatly in his jaws. "I deserved that!" he told himself as he enjoyed the titbit. Then, licking his lips, he again spoke to the crow on the branch.

"Silly crow. You're the ugliest bird I've ever seen, you have the worst voice I've ever heard, but most of all, you're the most stupid bird I've ever met! And thanks for the cheese." And off he trotted well satisfied with himself . . .

THE MOUSE AND THE LION

Once upon a time . . . a little mouse, scampering over a lion he had chanced upon, happened to wake him up. The angry lion grabbed the mouse and held it to his jaws. "Don't eat me, Your Majesty!" the mouse pleaded: "Forgive me! If you let me go, I'll never bother you again. I'll always be grateful, and will do you a good turn one day."

The lion, who had no intention of eating such a little scrap, and only wanted to frighten the mouse, chuckled: "Well, well. A mouse that hopes to do a lion a good turn! By helping me to hunt, maybe? Or would you rather roar in my place?" The mouse was at a loss for words. "Sire, I really . . ."

"All right. You can go," said the lion, shortly, opening his paw. The mouse scurried thankfully away.

Some days later, the lion fell into a trap and found he was caught fast in a stout net. Try as he might, he could not escape. And the more he struggled, the more he became entangled in the mesh, till even his paws were held fast. He could not move an inch: it was the end. His strength, claws and fearsome fangs gave him no help in freeing himself from the tangle. He was about to resign himself to a cruel fate when he heard a small voice: "Do you need help, Sire?"

Exhausted by his struggles, his eyes wet with rage, the lion looked round. "Oh, it's you! I'm afraid there's little you can do for me . . ."

But the mouse broke in: "I can gnaw the ropes. I have strong teeth and, though it will take me some time, I'll manage." So the little mouse quickly gnawed at the meshes and soon the lion tugged a paw free, then another, till he finally succeeded in working himself free of the net.

"You see, Sire," said the mouse, "I've done you a good turn in exchange for the favour you did me in letting me go unharmed."

"How right you are. Never before has a big animal like myself had to be so grateful to a little scrap like you!"

THE CONFERENCE OF THE MICE

Once upon a time . . . there was a large tabby cat which, from the minute she arrived at the farm, spread terror among the mice that lived in the cellar. Nobody dared go outside for fear of falling into the clutches of the awful cat.

The fast-shrinking mouse colony decided to hold a conference to seek a way of stopping themselves from becoming extinct. Taking advantage of the cat's absence one day, mice of all ages streamed into the conference room. And certain that they could solve the matter, each one put forward a suggestion, but none of the ideas were really practical.

"Let's build an outsize trap," one mouse suggested. When this idea was turned down, another said: "What about poisoning her?" But nobody knew of a poison that would kill cats. One young widow, whose husband had fallen prey to the ferocious cat, angrily proposed: "Let's cut her claws and teeth, so she can do no more harm." But the conference did not approve of the widow's idea.

At last, one of the mice, wiser than the rest, scrambled to the top of the lantern that shone over the meeting. Waving a bell, he called for silence: "We'll tie this bell to the cat's tail, so we'll always know where she is! We'll have time to escape, and the slow and weaker mice will hear her coming and be able to hide!"

A round of hearty applause met the wise mouse's words, and everyone congratulated him on his original idea.

". . . We'll tie it so tightly that it will never come off!"

". . . She'll never be able to sneak quietly up on us again! Why, the other day, she suddenly loomed up right in front of me! Just imagine . . ."

However, the wise mouse rang the bell again for silence. "We must decide who is going to tie the bell on the cat's tail," he said. There was not a sound in the room except for a faint murmur: "I can't, because . . ."

"Not me!" "I'd do it willingly, but . . ." "Neither can I . . ." "Not me!" "Not me!"

Nobody was brave enough to come forward to put the plan into action, and the conference of the mice ended without any decision being made. It's often very easy to have bright ideas, but putting them into practice is a more difficult matter . . .

THE DONKEY THAT THOUGHT
HE WAS CLEVER

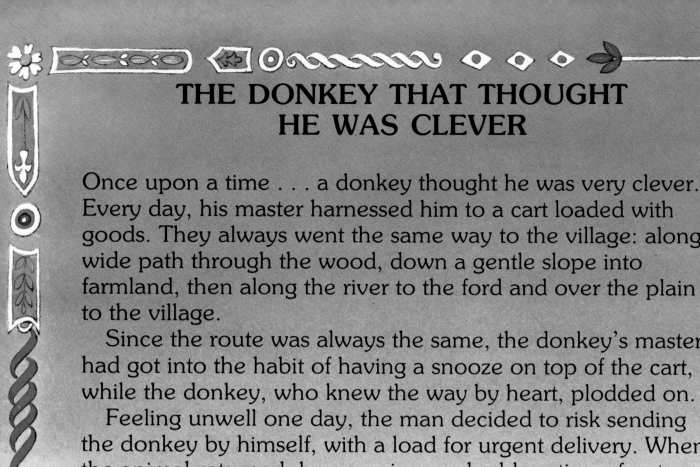

Once upon a time . . . a donkey thought he was very clever. Every day, his master harnessed him to a cart loaded with goods. They always went the same way to the village: along a wide path through the wood, down a gentle slope into farmland, then along the river to the ford and over the plain to the village.

Since the route was always the same, the donkey's master had got into the habit of having a snooze on top of the cart, while the donkey, who knew the way by heart, plodded on.

Feeling unwell one day, the man decided to risk sending the donkey by himself, with a load for urgent delivery. When the animal returned, he was given a double ration of oats as a reward.

"Since you're so clever at remembering the way," the man said, "I'm going to send you alone always, then I can do other jobs!" And from then on, in all kinds of weather, the donkey travelled to the village by himself. His master was delighted.

However, one morning, when the donkey reached the river, he decided to shorten his journey by wading across the water. But he entered the river at a deep spot, much deeper than the donkey expected, and he had to swim against the current.

Luckily, he was carrying a load of salt that day, and some of it dissolved in the water, easing the donkey's load, so that he reached the other side without much difficulty. "I am clever," said the donkey, pleased with himself. "I've found a short cut."

Next day, the man loaded the cart with sponges, and the donkey set off as usual. When he arrived at the river, he again thought he would take the short cut, and entered the water as he had done the day before. But this time, the sponges soaked up the water and made the cart heavy, so that the poor animal could not keep his head above water. And in spite of all his efforts, the donkey that thought he was so clever, sank below the surface of the water together with his load.

THE ANIMALS AND THE PLAGUE

Once upon a time . . . a terrible scourge swept through a huge forest, full of animals. It was the plague. One after the other, all the animals, big and small, strong and weak, died of the dreadful disease. None could hope to escape such a horrible fate, not even the lion himself, king of the forest. Indeed, it was the lion who gathered together the survivors, and said in a trembling voice: "This disaster is a punishment for our wicked ways. And I for one will admit I've been wicked. If you find me guilty, I'll gladly give up my life if you think that would help you in making amends for your own sins. So I confess that, during my lifetime, I've eaten many an innocent sheep."

"But, Sire," broke in one of the animals, "surely you don't think that eating sheep is a serious sin. We too . . . we too . . ." And they all began to tell their own stories.

One by one, the animals told of their crimes against their neighbours. The leopard had killed on more than one occasion, the eagle had snatched rabbits and lambs, the fox and the wolf had stolen and murdered. Even the placid-looking owl had little birds and mice on his conscience. Everyone had some wicked deed, serious or otherwise, to confess. But each animal, after his confession, was forgiven by the others, all just as guilty, of course. Last came the donkey, who said with a mortified air: "I did a very wicked thing too. One day, instead of just grazing here and there, I ate two clumps of grass in a clover meadow, without permission. I was sorry afterwards, and I've had a guilty conscience about it ever since!"

All the animals glared at the donkey and, shouting and calling insults, they chorussed: "So that's who brought the plague on us! Stealing grass from a poor peasant! Shame on you!" And the fate of the donkey was decided unanimously.

How often are innocent folk made to pay for the wicked deeds of the guilty.